MURDER
ON THE ICE FLOE IN
NASHVILLE

MURDER ON THE ICE FLOE IN NASHVILLE

JB CLEMMENS

ReadersMagnet, LLC

Murder on the Ice Floe in Nashville
Copyright © 2020 by JB Clemmens

Published in the United States of America
ISBN Paperback: 978-1-952896-95-8
ISBN eBook: 978-1-952896-96-5

This book is written to provide information and motivation to readers. Its purpose is not to render any type of psychological, legal, or professional advice of any kind. The content is the sole opinion and expression of the author, and not necessarily that of the publisher.

All rights reserved. No part of this publication may be reproduced, stored in a retrieval system or transmitted in any way by any means, electronic, mechanical, photocopy, recording or otherwise without the prior permission of the author except as provided by USA copyright law.

ReadersMagnet, LLC
10620 Treena Street, Suite 230 | San Diego, California, 92131 USA
1.619.354.2643 | www.readersmagnet.com

Book design copyright © 2020 by ReadersMagnet, LLC. All rights reserved.
Cover design by Ericka Obando
Interior design by Shemaryl Tampus

A robust slim infant was born to the Tilman's living in Tennessee. Momma cried out, not from pain but only inspiration, "I'm calling him Taper because he slid out so very easily like a thin candle." That was the start of a lucrative business for the Tilman family. Selling candles kept food on the table for Taper's first sixteen years. Mom's input, in addition to design of candles, extended to other products and the new name *Tilman's party fare*, which included fashionable fireworks.

Taper helped in the store until both his Momma and Papa died of food poisoning. Though he was suspected of causing that, no evidence was found to arrest him. Tainted apple butter from the local roadside stand was found. From then on he took over the business entirely with no sibling even volunteering. They knew his 'bull in a china shop' ways and didn't want to butt heads with him. Several employees quit too. He decided he needed an ally for work and Gaybelle Sand fit the bill nicely, A good girl and loyal employee, she packaged up the candles or fireworks to ship out. Taper hoped to seal up the alliance by eventually marrying her. On the side, a beautiful girl of loose moral values shared his bed. He fabricated excuses those nights to explain his absence at home. If Taper could have controlled that fox he'd have wed her, but he knew it wouldn't have worked in his favor.

After the Sand/ Tilman wedding in May, Gaybelle gave birth to a son they named Wick.

His birth or name did not ignite the spark of love Gaybelle hoped for with Taper and her disappointment in him grew.

Eighteen years later, Taper Tilman was found in the Cumberland River near Nashville. Around his neck was the fishing line he'd used on the ice floe, taut and twisted on the skin. A steelhead trout dangled from the Adam's apple. The busted up wood from the shelter and Styrofoam cooler were the only remnants from the sportsman's habitat. The harbormaster that first spotted the body called emergency for assistance and the police verified they were on their way.

Every police station has a radio band that is unique to its location. Berry Hill was near the Cumberland River and got the call about the body there. Sargent Tori Calhoun responded immediately with their arrival time and the usual warning about "hands off of the crime scene and body". Selecting valuable officer Stevie to ride along they headed to the squad cars. Stevie had stopped first at the officers' locker room to get her boots, as the river was near the record high.

"Get your horse going, girl," Sgt. Calhoun yelled out the window as the officer climbed in front.

Stevie apologized, "I'm sorry sir. Are you trying to be first to arrive?"

The Sargent didn't speak but gave Stevie a look that said, "I'm in charge so no questions." Relenting for friendship she added, "I'm stopping first to pick up the famous Lieutenant James who spoke last night for the police veterans donor organization."

"Oh wow. I read about his involvement arresting that filthy pedophile four years ago."

"'He's got a knack for finding clues. He is one of my MUST meet of people. Must is Maybe Useful Some Day. He's identified murderers in New York and even Tempe, Arizona. We do have to hurry but Wood knows how to run preliminary investigations if we're delayed."

"There he is now." James was easing out of a taxi on the right side a few hundred feet ahead. It would have been possible to jump from cab to squad car in a New York minute. However, Tori used the siren and waited for him to walk closer.

Eli James toted one bag and jumped in the back seat explaining that the siren troubled the Uber driver.

"He thought he did something illegal. I told him it was for me as I was suspected of not paying taxi drivers. His expression darkened so I told him it was a joke and gave him a generous tip."

The officers laughed and introduced themselves asking, 'How did everything go at the banquet for veteran donations, Lieutenant?

"The boys in blue showed up in record numbers. It was very pleasant. The Chicken Kiev tasted great though my usual trouble identifying condiments persisted. The Danish type dessert included apple butter sauce–only it was really prune. I had a bad experience with them once in Boy Scouts. The master of Ceremonies introduced me just after I took a bite. Trying to swallow the wretched taste in my mouth my greeting unfortunately came out, 'Welcome, venison and polecats' instead of veterans and police captains."

"How did they react? You essentially called them game meat or skunks."

Tori asked.

"Oh like Ricky Ricardo of The Lucy Show, I had some 'splaining to do fast. The talk went well enough though. Where are we headed now?"

The police officers chuckled through Eli's funny story then got to serious business.

Sargent Calhoun spoke first, "It's a drowning in the Cumberland River near the harbor. In fact, harbormaster Tug Richards telephoned about the body. He thinks he knows the man's identity, but we have to verify it in person. Almost there. The river is muddy. Clue from Luke Bryan, is 'better have your boots on'"

James indicated he did. All three of them were wearing squall or storm coats too.

> As they pulled into the harbor parking, it was hard to miss the giant sign:
>
> Fish on private float
> TUG'S COUNTRY FINE FISHING
> "Fishing here is the best, summer or winter" Travis Trask, country singer

"Fine endorsement from that popular singer", James interjected immediately.

Stevie, a country western fan asked if country music was big in New York.

James responded, "It could be bigger, though I like it fine. Why not?"

Stevie added, "Sgt. Calhoun is a singer here."

"Very interesting. Tell me more about it. Are you performing nearby? Popular?" Eli James inquired.

I'm not as popular as I wish. I'll tell you details later on. There's the harbormaster heading over to us.

Hands up in the air, Tug yelled, "Terrible thing. Not good for business. Or this poor guy either. Glad you're here though. Careful on the dock, it's still slippery. Don't want two bodies in the water."

Tug Richards was very well known in Nashville for the fishing spot but also for his great guitar playing often accompanying local artists or even strumming in his office. Sargent Calhoun had sung with him on occasion too. Though he enjoyed it, the harbor business earned the income needed to live.

"We need details, Tug. When, where especially how this happened."

"I don't sleep at the harbor, but I arrived at 5:45 this morning. He was floating around then. Fellow's name is Taper Tilman–paid for the whole night. Seemed capable of independent ice fishing and had means to get him to shore if necessary. I wasn't worried."

Sargent Calhoun asked, "Do we need to get someone to haul him out?"

Tug sized up the Lieutenant and decided the three of them could handle it without getting too wet doing it.

Tori observed the look he gave James and quickly introduced him.

"This is Lieutenant James from New York. He's quite famous in detective work."

A smiling Tug shook his hand and commented on the Wellington boots he had on. "Those look expensive, maybe not meant for getting wet?"

James replied, "They're waterproof to the knee. How deep is the water?"

"Near the dock under two feet."

"I'm here three more days. I can get new boots"

Sargent Calhoun picked up the chatter on her wrist radio. "There's no need for that. I had Wood call the ambulance. We need to verify the victim is dead not only in shock. And the coroner needs to certify that. Police have made mistakes on it before"

Tug went out toward the river in a rescue boat not needed very much, except emergency situations. Using a very long pole, he guided the body to the shore.

As Taper's drenched face came in closer, James remarked, "It's not shock. The purple neck, a sure sign of suffocation, means he is dead."

The ambulance got there turning off the sirens as two first responders and the medical examiner joined everyone at the dock. The medical examiner ruled it death by strangulation and the responders heaved the body out of the water and onto a gurney for transport.

James asked to check the victim's pocket and it was allowed.

While Gabby Kline coordinated the rescue or dive team, Lt. James and Sgt. Calhoun looked over the river and murder scene. "We can be sure of murder because of strangulation marks however the method of overcoming the victim is not known," James mused aloud. "Maybe a large enough boat had impact on the floe. Tori, what is over there by Tug's office?"

"Oh that's famous," She got very interested.

"The 656 mile long Tennessee Run of the Cumberland River tows barges of 45 to50 million tons of goods from the Ohio River confluence of Poor Fork annually. On the banks is Marine Discount towing and the well -known Ascend Amphitheater venue for famous country singers. The Mercy Lounge includes a river outlet, as does Ryman Auditorium, audible from the riverbanks. Popular spots, nights and most evenings., the ice hole fishing area is visible from all three."

"I'll check with the owners for remembered sounds from there."

"Good luck with it, James. The decibels from the music are loud enough."

⁂

"Maybe something very sizable, like a boat engine overrode the recording of the live show though," James suggested.

Tori added, "Last night was writer's night so not as crowded or loud. Tug's speedboat will take you over to talk to the owner soon."

"Great. Tori get Stevie and Wood on the radio station output last night. Taper had a transistor, now waterlogged, on the floe. See what he listened to and if there were any interruptions during the night. It's probably meaningless but I can't be sure."

"Okay"

"Also we need to check the bars near Tug's for fights or spillover into the fishing area…"

"Tug stayed up late and heard nothing."

"How late?"

"He says until 12."

"Usual bar closings at two?"

"Yeah except the Blue Room's open pretty much all night. They just close the steel sound impeding doors to allow campers to get shut eye."

"Who camps in this cold weather?"

"Lots of hardy Nashville folks around with high tech survival equipment usually used for hunting."

"Is there a way to track those hardy types on the river bank?"

Tori gave a twisted smile and said, "No not really, though they turn up for Rory's breakfast."

"Let's interview them. Later, I'm going walk down the river edge and observe outside the bar," James called back.

Officers Stevie and Wood took a speedboat to the Mercy Lounge Cannery Row nearby to check the river action of last night's scene. In fur-lined parkas and Sherpa insulated squall jackets, Tori and James travelled in Tug's twelve seat excursion motorboat to Roarin' Rory's on the River, the closest entertainment venue. It didn't take very long. In the distance they saw that the famous Blue Room arena wasn't closed up but doors were shut. However, "Roarin Rory" stood on the dock to greet the boaters, singing and playing last night's triumphs from successful songwriters. James exited the boat to the song playing…

> Stuck on thin ice
> Haul me in baby
> My heart is asking twice
> Free me and save me

Lt. James immediately asked, "Who wrote that one?"

Rory answered, "New one is from Russ Jensen. Crowd liked it. Good for Tug's business too."

"I see that would be," James replied.

Rory stopped singing to inquire, "How bout breakfasts now? There's toast."

※

"How does Darth Vader like his toast?"

Tori gave the straight line of 'I don't know' as Rory laughed impishly.

"On the dark side!"

"Skywalker hotcakes are ready on Dontui, soon here too. How many would you like to eat now? They're Kepler 16476 unusual pancakes. They discovered a new planet that orbits two suns, not Tatooine, a circumbinary planet. I've been watching the new Star Wars movie."

"It sure affected your imagination", Tori groaned.

"I hope not the cooking, Rory." James had visions of burnt toast and orange pancakes.

"No it's reality safe. Help yourself,"

"I'd like to know more information about Russ Jensen. The lyrics are intriguing. Maybe while we eat, you can fill us in."

James had a few pancakes and Tori took raspberry jam on top of toast to a nearby table. Rory joined them as he began talking.

Russ has talent but the draw now is his dog, Melody. It's quite a story about that. Jensen, like Elvis Presley entering the army, sang his goodbye beautifully on leaving for duty. Important recordings were made. Soon after, battle intervened causing critical shell shock events that left Russ's voice shattered. The dog found him. Gently licking his bruised neck, the dog felt a felt response—only a low guttural sound though. Amazingly, Melody matched it in pitch whining. The initial sound of howls became tunes pleasing to Jensen and he touched the dog, naming her Melody. As he healed, soon the inseparable singers entertained USO troops then returned home to America. Performing here now, magic wonders often happen as they sing together. It was as if it was meant to be. Here's a recording from October:

Rory took out his phone. Jensen writes the first part.

> I'm the melody
> For your part
> Joining each other
> Heart o Heart
> The dog formed the words
> The man couldn't express
> In velvet sound and chords
> On pitch in tune more or less
> "Here is with the dog singing along:"

James reacted, "It's quite remarkable. The kind of thing expected on The Jimmy Fallon Nightly Show."

He added, "It's not exactly a human voice but neither is a guitar, violin or keyboard. Melody's instrument is unique accompaniment. What is the magic wonder about, though?" James asked Rory.

"Oh that is hype or maybe hearsay. When they took the stage in a rainstorm it stopped suddenly and a woman in the crowd says clouds in the sky formed wings."

"Obviously other explanations are possible. Anything else happen when Jensen was last seen up on stage?"

"Yeah, it did. During their number, fireworks were scheduled, set off somewhere left of stage. It didn't go right. Members of the band said fiery sparks hit the dog's neck and she ran off. Russ didn't even finish the song and took off after her fast. They never came back that night. Odd thing is no one's seen them for three days."

"Is his residence nearby? Anybody try there?"

Rory backtracked, "Harlene Sted is close to him though she hasn't seen him either. Her brother is a friend. They both sing, though Cody's not too successful. He went over there. Nobody answered the door and Russ's Harley wasn't parked out in front."

"The dog rides on the back?"

"Oh yeah, usually. She's a very talented dog."

James further explained, "I'm returning to New York but Sgt. Calhoun will take over investigating and finding them. Right now murder is a priority."

"I heard what happened at Tug's. Taper wasn't exactly Andy Griffith of Mayberry that everybody liked but also didn't deserve violent death. Nobody does unless they've done heinous crimes themselves. I guess the jury is still out for Tilman's past though."

"We'll find out if that's true. Thanks Rory, I enjoyed the delicious pancakes but we've got an ongoing investigation. Lots of things to do now." James gave a nod Sgt. Calhoun's way and they left immediately.

On the way to the river, a couple came up to Tori, grinning.

"We enjoyed your Kane Brown song very much the other night. Well, you sounded exactly like his voice. How do you do it?"

"I usually just sing what I hear. Actually it's a gift I'm grateful for."

"Ever do old Luke Bryan hits? I love Rollercoaster."

"So glad you enjoyed my music. I like all of Luke's hits too. There's not much call for voice matching in the Grand Ole Opry now though it's welcome at bars. I'm doing Trish Yearwood's" "She's in Love with the Boy next time. Like it?"

"Oh that's super. We'll be there early. Thanks Tori."

James guided Tori onto the pathway overlooking the river as the complementary twosome turned toward Roaring Rory's for food.

"Your fan club?" James winked an eye.

"Something like it and I'm glad to have it. Living in this crazy town, it's very easy to get lost in obscurity given the number of superstars performing everywhere. Having just one person appreciate what you do is meaningful, even encouraging. Hey that was two of them. My career is skyrocketing." She pointed up, rolled her eyes and laughed.

"You've still got law enforcement waiting in the wings. I'd like hearing you sing–Bitsy too especially. She's on New York Philharmonic's Board of Directors, enjoys country music's easy flow too. Once I caught her in the kitchen singing along to Nobody But You".

"The new Blake Shelton/ Gwen Stefani one?"

"That's right. I think she favors his new wife over the other one, though they're both good singers."

"True, only different styles or lyrics. James, I'm troubled about the dog and Russ Jensen. Rory told me that Tug befriended them when they first got back to America. I'm going to talk to him. Also I saw a boat rental shop nearby that I want to investigate for last night rentals or disappearances."

"It's a good idea, Tori. I'm going to walk the riverside toward that bar I see up in the distance for investigating too. Hope we find something helpful. I'll meet you at Tug's in an hour or so."

"Make it two."

"Sure, that's good."

Lt. James had one day visiting in Nashville. He thought about Bitsy, the rich widow who'd become his soul mate in life. Though she was in New York now he felt her presence as he walked gingerly on the riverside. The bar in the distance appeared larger with each stride

MURDER ON THE ICE FLOE IN NASHVILLE

until he made out the sign in front, Raging Ruby's. Bitsy might be up for that entertaining nightlife with him if the music was good. It was soundless and still now though.

He picked up a section of pipe normally used to propel fireworks canisters and used it to determine the mud depth in front of him. He didn't want to be up to his Wellingtons in "suck you in" thick goo. Being very careful, he saw nothing at first. He discovered that only looking down didn't help his quest as much as scanning the bank ahead for possible partygoers inadvertent discards. He found, among zip tabs, cups and usual smoking butts, cherry bombs, old roman candles and unexploded fireworks for which he had no explanation unless they were duds. James kept one for testing later on. Under the cartridge he found a treasure of sorts. Nestled in the indentation was an opaque medallion. He wasn't sure if it was money so he used a tissue to wipe it clean. No dollar amount was given but there was this motto:

> "First, carry the load"

There was movement outside the bar. A woman dressed in jeans, boots and an old army khaki flak jacket was setting trash in a barrel. James called tentatively, "Ruby?"

Standing up she laughed and shouted, "There is no Ruby. I'm the owner, Harlene. Who is asking?"

James moved in closer saying, "I'm Lieutenant James, working with Sgt. Tori Calhoun on a nearby murder case."

"Murder now? Or only a drowning?" "Actually both—a guy murdered in Tug's ice fishing dock last night. Did you see or hear anything out of the ordinary, unusual? Sorry that's redundant."

"Not sure what redundant means but our bar was lively enough to bury sound or the dead." "Oh, I see. May I check the trash?"

"Looking for clues? You'll only find cigarette butts, used pyrotechnics and uneaten food. Help yourself though."

"I believe I'll take your word for that. Thanks."

James held out the circular medallion he'd found on the shore. "Have you ever seen something like it, Harlene?"

She glanced down and exclaimed, "Oh my, my husband used to carry one. It's a reminder for remembering that soldiers often carry the load for us, including fallen servicemen. How did you find that?"

"Observing primarily. I tend to study everything, even the ordinary to not overlook what might eventually be significant. Your husband is active military?"

"No, Lieutenant, it's a sad story."

"I'm a good listener…"

"After an exciting Garth Brooks concert, I met this most interesting man–great looking and kind of heart, on leave from army duty. For two weeks we enjoyed everything two lovers do. His promise of marriage I took as gospel after leave duty was over. We corresponded often after he returned to the army. It became clear it wasn't the usual flimsy empty promise of some soldiers on leave. I was seventeen and in a month I learned I was pregnant, Hank wrote of his joy in it and even listed me as beneficiary for army veterans insurance policy."

"He was killed in battle right after that."

"I'm so sorry, Harlene," James quietly expressed.

"He was never my husband but I think of him that way even now."

"Lt. James, Who was murdered? Do you know?"

James straightened up to his full six feet and answered immediately, "A man named Taper Tilman." He fixed his eyes on Harlene's facial expression on hearing it. First reactions often told him valuable information about relationships.

"Taper is dead… Nobody told me if they even knew. It's terrible news."

James noted that Harlene looked immediately down and left on answering. Often that indicated a telling sign of insincerity or perhaps thinking of dust-to-dust idea.

"You knew him?"

"You'll find out easily enough that we were… she hesitated enough that James noticed, …close." "Then it must be a shock. We'll talk about it later on."

While James talked outside with Harlene, a man in his twenties stood in the doorway, arms over his head and bracing the frame.

"Sis, George won't give me a beer unless you okay it. What is that shup now?"

He shouted now, "I am twenty-five. That guardianship thing is over."

"It's okay Cody," she motioned a thumbs up to the bartender standing close to Cody inside. "I'm not trying to run your life, just a bar. LCB was snooping around yesterday that's all. You look nineteen in the morning and we don't need them running your license either."

Cody turned inside for his beer, returning with it saying, "If you want worries, try finding Russ and Melody. I hope they're okay."

"Oh me too. Cody, this is Lieutenant James, a New York detective working the case, Taper's murder included, along side Sgt. Calhoun here in Nashville."

"Taper is dead?" He spat out some beer, and then turned to James. "Nice to meet you especially if Russ is found safe from the effort of police."

James' first impression, that Cody was trouble and rude, got revised to caring and respectful. Some circumstances indicated that the young man might not BE trouble though he was IN trouble somehow.

"I'm returning to New York. Are you open, willing to consider a suggestion?"

"Sure if it helps"

"Telephone or visit veterinary hospitals in the area."

"It's sensible, sir. Melody's injuries were probably severe enough. Knowing Russ he'd want to be wherever she is. Thank you."

James started to go back to Tug's for meeting Calhoun, but Harlene touched his arm saying. "My brother is not an alcoholic. A beer or two helps him forget past nightmares then he switches to Rockstar or Seven-up and works very hard helping me in the bar all afternoon or some nights. I just needed to explain the morning drinking."

"There's no need Harlene. 'I learned the Monsters Ain't the Ones Beneath the Bed' from Eric Church. Everybody has ways of fighting them."

※※※

…James inspected the fireworks cabinet as he studied everything new, not overlooking the ordinary or what might eventually be significant. Just then a burly man entered toting sound equipment left in the backroom.

His deep voice resonated. "Your friends didn't pick up after themselves, Harlene!"

"I know it, Griz. Things are someone else's toys to him when it's time to put everything away."

"We're expecting the lunch crowd in there two hours from now. It's a mess."

"I'll speak to him about it but I doubt much will ever change."

"He's got no idea how to treat things let alone a woman. Up to me, I wouldn't let him near the place ever. I know what I'd do to him if he tried."

"Griz, for me, don't get edgy. He had enough of a chokehold on you. It doesn't matter, he's dead now."

Griz face didn't register surprise and he spoke up, "Now that's GOOD news."

With a grunt and a swift turn he went back in back.

It was the kind of information James stored for use later on without letting on he heard it. Instead he turned to Harlene nearby and inquired about the bar food menu.

"Help yourself to the placemat menu or takeout one, everything's on both. Are you staying for lunch?"

"No, but the Sargent and assisting police officers will want something for dinner later on. I'd like to treat them here."

"That's mighty nice. The food is good and reasonable. Band starts evening performance at five o'clock, Jimmy Buffett time."

"Great, it's five clock somewhere here then?"

"Yep. You got it. Till then, take care."

"Other than your relationship, was Tilman involved with anyone else who resented him? I'm not saying you had issues, just wondering who had motive for killing him."

"You're gonna find that Taper had enemies. Well, first there's his only son, Wick. He resents how mother floundered after the divorce. Taper cut him out of business dealings too."

"What about this Griz guy now?"

"Oh, that's insignificant in considering murder. Taper has–had this super classic Viper sports car indulgence and he parked it wherever he wanted to usually. I had vinyl tablecloths laid out for drying and he put the Viper on top of them. Griz saw I was upset and just picked the car up and moved it off of them. Some tie rod damage occurred and Taper threatened to retaliate and sue Griz. Nothing much actually happened though."

Sargent Calhoun navigated the slippery slope to the dock of Chase's Boat Rentals thinking that it was quicker than using the staircase further down. Suddenly though she found herself sliding down on her back toward the river until this strong arm grabbed both of her wrists and pulled her upright and into the boat he stood firmly in.

"There's a staircase, you know" a pleasant voice said without sounding overly judgmental.

"Well first, thank you and second, I wanted to get a glance at these idle boats before I searched for the owner here."

"You've got both now. I'm owner Jamie Chase and this tugboat is a Weedo 4" that sells for $5000 or rents for $50 a day. What features are you looking for?"

Tori felt sensations at being near one extremely handsome man though experienced police training kicked in fast.

"I'm here for a murder investigation, Mr. Chase" She extended her hand firmly, "Sargent Calhoun of Metropolitan Police in Davidson County. A man named Taper Tilman was strangled following the break-up of the ice floe at Tug's fishing place. It's possible a tugboat was used."

"I'm surprised as all get out, ma'am. First, that our police are so pretty and that Tilman got whacked now. Murder's not too common around here."

"Well the owner at Rory's heard a tugboat around the time we estimate the murder to have been. Are all of your tugs accounted for between 2 and 3 am?"

"Oh yes officer (he emphasized the title use omitting Sargent designation, though)" Rory has one himself even, so he would know the sound of it—but everything is right as rain here. I'm Jamie. Mr. Chase is too formal.

"Jamie, then, is a tug capable of ramming or destroying the ice Tug uses? They could. These little babies suffice for all sorts of fishing, towing and sometimes even sunbathing." Tori countered the uncomfortable feeling that he was picturing her now in a bathing suit by envisioning filing of daily reports.

"You said Rory has a tugboat."

"Yeah a mini Weedo 4" aluminum, no horn model."
"Does anyone else here on the river own one that you know of?"

"There are three. Tug has two, pretty obvious huh?"

"Who is the other one?" "Harlene Sted. Actually she brought it here for service this morning."

"What's wrong with it?"

"The engine's fine but the tiller isn't functioning. Something stuck under the housing. Easy fix." "Well don't. It could be evidence. I'll have someone in the department come get it. Nobody else?"

I caught a glimpse of an older man going past on the river. I don't know him though. There are other marinas that sell or rent them.

"Okay, I'll check. If I may ask one thing, though… If the tiller wasn't working how did Harlene get the boat over here without using it?" "Now you're pretty smart. Most usual cops wouldn't think to ask that. She used an old piece of wood and only slowest speed." "Do you still have it?" "I can't imagine why anyone would want it but it's in the trash barrel near the shop. I'll get it,"

While Jamie fetched the wood, Tori estimated the distance between the various places on the side of Chase's shop and Tug's where the murder occurred. Not far. There was a bar on down the river about only one mile away. Probably James would investigate it on his walk up the shore. Rory's was down from this place and three other places were visible though she didn't expect much help from them, they looked locked up and probably were only open in the summer. She'd check anyway.

On past Chases' Tori found a shack with no sign outside identifying it. It could be deserted, however smoke from something curled out the back of an attached building. She decided to venture closer. On the shack front was a visible window with a sign.

"Knock for me."

Of course she did. No one answered but on her left she heard the sound of boots stomping. A very short woman was stepping forward in hip boots carrying five pieces of wood in various lengths, and all edges ragged.

"Do you need help?" Tori called out instinctively.

"Oh no, thanks. May I help you?"

From the accent used, Tori guessed the woman wasn't native to America, though her English sounded good enough. She didn't want to frighten her but suspected the police uniform already had.

"There was trouble last night over at Tug's. Did you hear any noise?"

"You're police, now right?"

"I admit it yes. You're not in trouble though. I'm Sargent Calhoun from Metro. Your name is…"

"Thomasina. Only to locals and customers, Tommy."

"Last name? Sorry it's procedure."

"Salgado de Castillo y Rojas is my full name."

"Since it's murder I'm investigating, I appreciate it."

"Muerte! Not Tug?"

"No. We believe someone used a boat to demolish the wood scaffolding and ice the victim sat on then eventually strangled the guy." Thomasina immediately dropped the wood she held.

"And I'm holding evidencia"

Tori had to admit she was quick enough in making the connection.

"I just gathered free floating firewood." "Okay, I'll check it later on. Maybe you know the victim–Taper Tilman."

If ever Calhoun saw a look of fright and malice mixed, it was on that woman's face. Thomasina quickly replaced it with an inscrutable blank one.

"He's known around here, or was. Come inside the store. It's warmer there."

Tori knew a diversionary tactic when she saw one but that's the way it was with suspects or even innocent people who didn't want to reveal information. On the way, she examined the five pieces of wood, probably from Tug's, and seeing nothing important, left them for the lab.

She caught up with Thomasina just inside a side door, entering a merchandise world usually only found in foreign markets. Souvenirs, hats, sunglasses and bags of salty snacks hung on the wall on the left. Decals, key chains, rosaries and waterproof boxes sat opposite that. Near the cash register was a bin holding lots of flip-flops and beer on the shelves behind it. Not that surprising, there were no labels, sizes or even price tags on most of the items and Tori wondered if the owner expected haggling like in third world countries. Though the store's conglomeration was fascinating she got back on track to investigating.

"So, Thomasina, you knew Taper Tilman?" "He was a very mean man. Oh Dios Mio. It isn't right 'hablar mal de el muerte."

Tori's Spanish was good enough to recognize "speak ill of the dead" and she knew the woman would not elaborate now. She couldn't rule her out as a suspect but neither could she take Thomasina's dislike of the man for solid evidence. She might find the reason later on. Right now Tori's interest was sunglasses, just the right shade of purple that would shield her eyes from snow glare. She'd left hers in the squad car, which Stevie now had.

"Those are nice ones," the owner jumped in, "for only $5."

"Sold, Thomasina." Calhoun took out a five but said, "Cinco?"

"Ah senorita has traveled in Spanish speaking countries."

"Well just one. That was great fun. Thanks. Where were you on Friday night?"

"I was here."

"The whole night?"

"Yes"

"If you remember noise or events that could aid the police investigation, here's my number."

"Not likely. I wear a pair of these." She held up noise cancelling earphones.

She gave Thomasina the card and put on the sunglasses.

"Fantastico, Muy bien. Vaya con Dios."

Though the decking on the way to Tug's was slippery, Tori's boots had good tread. She passed a restaurant, Kayak rental store, and free fiberglass port-a-john, though the first two weren't open. She considered the third momentarily but remembered Tug had a restroom, nice fireplace and other amenities, so moved on. Flashing lights ahead caught her attention now. They cut off as she approached but the men, visible in boats were obviously official investigators. Picking up the pace, Calhoun caught up with the nearest one.

"Permission to board, sir, I'm Sargent Calhoun."

"Oh sure, hop in. We're structural forensic engineering officers, trying to reconstruct the crime scene by examining the demolished remains now." "Anything significant?"

"Whatever rammed into this ice floe hit on two diagonals, compromising the stability inherent in the scaffolding. We can't explain what happened to the ice itself since it's been melted or relocated by the natural river current."

"I see, interesting. Where is Tug, the owner, now?"

"He went inside the office to warm up. I'll go alongside the dock for you to go inside too."

"What's your name?"

"Earl Lembrooke"

"Nice to know you, Earl. I have a question about something. When Tilman was fishing, wouldn't he have heard a boat approaching fast upon the floe and got out of the way? He must have had a vehicle for leaving because the platform was out far from shore."

"Okay, two possibilities—we found shattered pieces of a one man pedal boat and headphones floating downriver. If he was listening to a game or music that would explain not hearing an approaching boat. When it got real close, though, not. It's possible the murderer took out the escape boat first before the victim could even react. It's hard to say, not being a witness."

Though the body was in the coroner's office, evidence was here for reconstructing of the crime, though much of that had floated away in the current.

A familiar voice said, "There is another possibility."

"James," Tori turned to the speaker, "What is your suggestion?"

"It's actually fact. I telephoned the examiner. They found a drug in the victim's body—opioid-type essentially—enough for confusing or immobilizing someone. Whether Tilman chose to take it or not is the question though."

"Also found this photograph." Earl handed an envelope to Tori. "It's wet of course though even when it dries, facial recognition would not work very well."

James inspected it. "It appears to be of a young girl from the outline of the face."

"We thought so too at first. It's hard to say, again"

"Well thanks, Earl. That's good work, to quote Gibbs."

As they talked, Tug walked out and offered everyone 'hot beverages' and fireplace warmth inside. James and Tori accepted immediately though the forensic experts, except Earl, declined, being in waterproof rubber suits, anxious to get back to the office and into comfortable clothes. Inside, couches surrounded the large fireplace, inviting and warm. There was a young man, in his twenties, already sitting off to the left. James and Tori did not recognize him though he resembled a photograph of Tilman.

Tug explained to everyone, "This is Wick Tilman, Taper's son. I called him. Hard thing, but I felt it was the right thing to do." A respectful silence was followed by handshakes of sympathy and condolence.

Wick spoke first, "Good to know the police are involved to solve everything. I called Mom, but she's not capable of making funeral arrangements or even talking to police. Her world narrowed after the divorce. Anyway, I'm here now if you have questions."

James spoke up immediately, "Did your father ever use drugs?" "Not that I know of… but then." "You remembered something?" James continued.

"Dad kept to himself usually. He wasn't a junkie but I wouldn't know if he used them recreationally or medicinally. Wasn't strangulation the cause of death, not drugs."

Wick seemed suddenly interested in his father's death more than before. For some reason, James didn't want to continue talking about the drugs with Wick. Perhaps it was sympathy for the young man or more likely he needed to investigate further before going on questioning him. James also considered what Wick shouted out to Tug as he left the fireplace haven.

"Sorry about your fishing business, Tug. If you want I'll help rebuilding the framework or replacing the pedal boat, if insurance won't cover everything."

Tug answered from in the kitchen, "Thanks that's not necessary. I spoke to my agent. Everything's fully covered. Take care of your mother instead, Wick."

On the couch, James turned to Calhoun, "Nice of Tug to show kindness to the kid."

"Tug's nice to everybody. He knows a lot of good and bad things about every local resident, but usually treats everyone the same fair way. He's a good guy."

Tug came out of the kitchen several times apparently setting out some sort of buffet. Tori admired the intent though laughed slightly at what men often considered entertainment foods. He set out:

> Pickles (still in jar)
> A package of crackers not opened
> A jar of olives (not in bowl)
> Cocktail sausages in a bowl this time
> Bag of chips
> Tub of Helluva Good Dip, lid off
> A hunk of cheese, a hunting knife for cutting
> Several plates of fine bone china to eat from
> A roll of paper towels

James smiled but understood. His Bitsy was not a whiz about cooking. Being rich, she was used to having someone else do that. He did wonder about the expensive china incongruous with the rest, though let it go without inquiring.

Earl, who'd taken off the insulated river clothes, had no qualms about the food display as he filled a plate and even got seconds. Tug came out, took and filled a plate himself. After he sat down to eat, James considered that it was the right time to find out some things. In his experience, food loosened the tongue of those who were eating provided they had enough in their stomachs first.

"Tug, thanks for the food. You seem of the 'live and let live' type, not a gossip monger or telling tales out of school that harm other people, but this is a police investigation. I'd appreciate knowing about people on the river. How you know isn't as important as the facts are."

"Well, I'll try. Hold on for one minute." Tug sat his plate on the floor and stood up. He walked to the kitchen and returned with a six-pack of longneck beers, twisting off a cap and taking a big swallow.

"Help yourself," he said humming John Pardi and Thomas Rhett's hit, "Ain't nothing that a Beer can't fix"

Tori and James shook their heads, citing work obligations, but Earl took a beer eagerly saying, "My shift is over for the day."

"Who's first on your list?"

"Tell us what you know, in any order, about Rory, Thomasina, Harlene and Cody Sted and Jamie Chase. Also Russ Jensen and certainly Taper Tilman."

"Rory is successful enough and he encourages aspiring musicians/songwriters to perform in Roarin' Rory's. As you said, I'm not a gossip though it's a fact he has them sign open contracts that may or may not benefit their future interests. That kinda verges on gossip though. His breakfasts are fabulous famous around here. He's no man of the year—I guess though he's a good businessman."

"Thomasina knows people need things on the river and sells accordingly. She is a devoted mother and Catholic for that matter. Once she asked me to put locks on her private entrance, like someone frightened her. She is a good person though not accepted by everyone because she's foreign."

"Jamie Chase has been here five years, only it's a sad story before that. He's from a very small town nearby in Texas—from a good family, only poor. He sang in choir and got singled out as soloist.

MURDER ON THE ICE FLOE IN NASHVILLE

He became very popular singing country songs at family gatherings, weddings and eventually headlined at the county fair. A talent scout happened by and offered Chase a recording studio contract, and a featured appearance in Nashville's Grand Ole Opry. Pretty excited, parents, cousins, uncles and townspeople scrapped up the money for plane and other travel expenses. The town went all out celebrating the send off. When he got to Nashville, there was no recording studio and Grand Ole Opry never heard of him. It turns out Tilman was behind it. He had taken on managing the near bankrupt Twanger Studio thinking it could be turned into profit. However the amount he paid for it didn't cover old creditors and they took everything for debts. It was his idea to lure a singer with empty useless promises never intending to honor them. He used up the travel expenses money for so called recording contract fees and still Twanger went belly up. Chase was near bankruptcy himself."

"Not a pretty story. How did he get from near poverty to a success in business?"

"After he got over being madder than a wet hen, he found a farm job up near the Tennessee River. I reckon you don't grow up where he did without being skilled using farm machinery. 'Six months on a farm 'fore he saved up'. That's a lyric from 'There was this girl' by Riley Green. When he arrived back here, he wanted nothing to do with Music City and singing."

"So he never sings anymore?" Tori asked.

"He relented once or twice in Bluebird Cafe–well received enough, though no big time offers. It takes time usually despite what fans think. Overnight sensation is very rare. It's a right time right place type thing."

"Did he ever confront or threaten Tilman?"

"No, not that I know of." Tug moved on to Russ Jensen, again skipping Harlene. James and Tori noticed but said nothing about it.

Tug began, "If I had a son, I'd want that to be Russ. He tackles work enthusiastically, shows kindness to every person he's around, and is very talented–some hard knocks like losing family in the 2018 tornado. They were included in 31 people killed when the EF3 twister touched down northeast of Nashville. Russ joined the army soon after." Tori told Tug they knew from Rory of the story of how Russ and Melody joined forces.

Tug summed it up in saying, "All I can say is God help anyone who hurt or tried to separate that dog from Russ."

"Now about Rory, since you brought him up, he's the happy host most of the time, tending bar and serving up breakfast but he has a darker side inside. Russ did not even like him for some reason and I value Russ's opinion on that. Until Russ is found you can't ask him, though."

"That leaves only Harlene and Cody, Tug. Is something significant about them?"

Once again Tug skipped over Harlene.

"You don't have to look very far to see tragedy in Cody's life. {He told the story of the accident. Though Cody pleaded not guilty saying he was drugged unknowingly, the result was not good. An eleven-year-old girl hospitalized for weeks swayed the judge. I've always had one question. Why did Tilman even let Cody drive that day? Tilman claimed he knew the kid had had one beer though knew nothing about drug use. Tilman paid for the girl's hospital bill and visited the parents. Cody fulfilled court sanctions and began to feel normal again until he went to sing in a benefit for Special Olympics. He was booed off the stage. The crowd read about the girl being struck down with him in the driver's seat. Can't blame them, though Cody's life don't amount to a hill of beans right now."

"Harlene, Tug—We need to know about Harlene." Tori recognized that tender look immediately. Though James had more of a man's reaction, he noted the deep feeling on Tug's face.

"I don't know where to start…" Tug's voice hesitated.

"How bout where you first met her." Suggested James.

"Okay that's easy. I talked to her in church. I'm not a regular goer, but the river swell and flooding of three years back made me think I needed to be grateful that everyone survived it. She sang one verse of Amazing Grace in a solo with the choir. It was beautiful and I complimented her when the service was over. We talked for a while, finding the Cumberland River one thing in common, and eventually walking back together. Unlike now, she seemed very happy."

"What's wrong now?"

"Something's troubling her. Last Friday she was sitting on the riverbank, head down in thought. I stopped and asked, 'Everything okay, Harlene?' She lifted up the hood of the jacket covering her eyes that were wet in tears, and replied, "Not everything is, but I'm fine. How are you, Tug?" We exchanged usual pleasantries but I sensed a need for privacy and

I left. If you ask me, it's Tilman causing the trouble. He bought the bar for her and used that to lord it over her. He insisted she perform songs in there and other venues too. Griz told me the other bars were sleazy types and Harlene often got hit on. Tilman ignored it and kept on pushing her. Griz didn't like that and the way Tilman oversaw things and threatened her sexually. It's a blessing he's gone from her life now—and Cody's too—no love lost there."

Tori Calhoun and Lt. Eli James were used to sorting through information obtained to find out what's important to the case. They thanked Tug and took off in different directions for meeting later on at Ruby's. Tori headed to the police station for finding out any new information and James stopped in a Rory's for clues why Russ Jensen didn't like the guy. From talking to patrons he learned very little but from investigating under the bar he found something interesting. His searching fingers found a three-pronged hook under the bar counter four stools apart. His surprised face attracted the attention of a woman sitting nearby.

"They're for purses—handy things. Who wants to hold onto the purse if drinking?"

She introduced herself saying, "I'm Joan and a regular here"

"Good to know you, Joan. I'm Lieutenant James. You're law enforcement too. Right?"

"You must be a fine detective. How did you know? I'm off duty."

"From your boots, standard regulation ones from Metro. Officers Stevie and Wood wear them. Also I saw the glint of a badge in your hooked purse." "I know Wood Tucker. Is that who you mean?"

"Yes. He's helping investigate purse hooks as I am." "All the bars have them," Joan told him, "except one here in Nashville–Cahoonas."

James raised an eyebrow at the name's implication.

"Yeah, it's a bar that limits gender. Anyway, I was riding with the neighborhood patrolman when their bartender summoned help. These two guys, I call them Frick and Frack to protect identities, caused trouble. Frick came in and switched bar stools because one had a rip in the seat. Frack who'd been sitting there was at the jukebox playing Rednecker (than you) from Hardy. Both men ordered Bud Lites. There was only one in the cooler so the bartender set it up on the bar to get one from the back. Fiery verbal slinging erupted in a fistfight for the one beer. Frick, to counter Frack's Rednecker, played "Country Boy Can Survive then" "Get off my Cloud" Still fighting, an ashtray and a whiskey glass got thrown at the jukebox. That's when the bartender called in police. Property damage had exceeded $4000. They ended up with disturbing the peace and vandalism charges, fines only and restitution. Cahoonas isn't the kind of place that bans men when their machismo is violent. They don't disallow woman either but females know better and avoid it."

"Do you know of Cody Sted?"

"I sure do, we dated"

"Tell me about him if not too painful."

"No pain, just usual break-up memories. When Cody got involved with music, his smooth voice and natural ability impressed listeners limited to Ruby's and a few other bars. In Nashville, 'Crazy Town' rules applied. It's "everybody plays, everybody sings" from Jason Aldean lyrics. Managers were everywhere but the paradox existed for needing success to get a good one and needing a good manager to be successful. The slamming door of agents was all too familiar to Cody. Then Taper Tilman stepped in and offered assistance out of friendship for Harlene and her brother. The Tilman name was known in this town enough, although for other reasons, some not very good, but still known. Taper had no experience in managing, though. The first, somewhat ineffective thing he did was to buy a vending company that serviced jukeboxes. Cody didn't see the logic of that but Tilman's "my way/highway" attitude was inflexible. Cody agreed to ride along on the routes between each bars' jukeboxes and learn to operate them. Tilman wasn't very patient, only critical and sarcastic. It didn't take very long for Cody to start ordering a beer to cope. Then it was one in each bar they visited. His "new manager" didn't discourage it, in fact even brought him one at Rory's. More than a couple now popular artists got started singing at Roarin Rory's On the River. Cody had hopes on that day but it wasn't meant to be. He told me he'd forever remember what happened next as ruining his life not the start of something good."

"What happened that's not good?"

"One day, my partner and I responded to a report of an accident on Sycamore Street near here. An eleven-year-old girl was injured and the ambulance was already there for her. I gave support to the paramedics while Ian, my partner dealt with the occupants of the car responsible for her injuries. When the ambulance sped off to the hospital I walked over to assist Ian. The driver, now being arrested was disoriented mumbling in slurred speech. It was Cody. Tilman was out of the passenger seat and appeared fine. I'd never seen Cody in that state of intoxication before. I had to admit it looked bad. Cody recognized me enough to shoot a look of anger my way. Another squad car showed up and the officers took him to the magistrate's office for arraignment. Once I thought I was in love with him but didn't love him very much now. I still gave support but he was the one who broke it off saying he couldn't endorse my job."

"It's difficult overlooking a mate's weakness, that's true. Anything else about that accident?"

"Just that the whole incident didn't seem right even. Can't say what that is but something seemed odd."

"Thanks, Joan. Enjoy your day. I'm heading to Raging Ruby's now. I'll say hello to Officer Wood from you."

"Thanks"

Stevie caught up with Tori and Eli James at Ruby's.

"Any clue from visiting the Mercy Lounge?" James asked.

Stevie spoke first, "Only two patrons admitted knowing Tilman slightly with no knowledge of his activities last night. Mornings, though, bars aren't open to lively conversations of the nighttime. The bar is a nice place to eat anytime it seemed. We noticed people enjoying themselves." "Did you ask if anyone from last night heard noises outside?"

Wood nodded adding, "Of those people who were inside last night only one heard engine sounds from the river direction. Guy named Hank Abrams, who sells machinery, heard something odd." "What did he think it was?"

"At first a boat, then it was vibration or low pitched moan that only lasted a minute or two then a boat engine gradually moving further up the river." "Did Hank say 'up the river exactly' or down?"

"I'm pretty sure he said up. I have notes. I'll check it." Wood pulled out his phone and read it. "Yep, up is right."

"Okay thanks. Anything else go on?"

"Well one strange thing. An over twenty-one year old girl, found a purse on the under bar hook when she was hanging hers there. The bartender saw our uniforms and gave it to us. I brought it here."

"Hum, not expensive. Is it empty?" "Practically empty. There's only lint, loose tobacco and one pill capsule, broken, but empty."

"No money or ID?" I've never known a woman to abandon her bag, forget it sometimes yes, not ditch it entirely.

"Nope nothing. What should we do with it?" "Give it to the lab. They might find useful information involving drug traffic from the pill capsule."

"I hope they don't find it's a 'roofie' or poison."

"We've got one unsolved crime that's enough."

"Got that right, sir. I'll take it to the lab now." "Good. Just ignore people staring at a man who is carrying a purse."

"Actually it's fashionable these days, probably not in Nashville."

"That's a given."

<hr />

Stevie caught up with Tori and James later at Raging Ruby's.

"They finally tracked down the owner of the purse from Mercy. She explained her bar hopping and shopping trip alright enough but could not account for the drug in the purse she abandoned."

"What is the last bar she visited before ending up at Mercy Lounge?" "Roarin Rory's. She searched in the old purse for ID before going inside and swears nothing funky was in there. The new purse came from Thomasina's inventory after that."

Tori put it together, "So the drug was introduced either at Thomasina's or in Rory's."

"I agree with that," James confirmed. "Stevie go to Rory's and question the bartender now."

"Why only the bartender?"

"I noticed his excessive cleaning underneath the bar on the customer side at breakfast. It was clean already. Do you have a photo of the woman, what's her name?" "Bebe Gunner."

"You're kidding!"

"No, that's the name on her driver's license. I have a copy of it for showing the bartender."

"Anybody know his name now?" "Where is Wood?" "In the men's room."

Eerily enough, Wood appeared immediately behind them and spoke, "The bartender's name is Judd, last name Stiles. He's one weird guy, Won't let me sit in the bar's corner, using the excuse it's hard for him to reach, then a woman comes in and he allows her to sit there." "It's probably your sex is just wrong," the Lieutenant offered. "Wood you should inquire at Thomasina's about the new purse."

Though Wood and Stevie were still on the clock, Tori was now officially off duty. James had been given freedom from the police chief to record and get reimbursed for consulting. He kept track in a notebook. He entered "free time" as of now.

"How bout singing right now, Tori?" He asked. "I'm leaving soon for New York."

James thought Tori would be flustered though he was wrong. She stood up and talked to Kip, the band's guitarist for a minute than the music began. Tori dug right in picking up with the lively instrument's enthusiasm.

> 'She was in the backyard
> Say it was a little past nine
> When her prince pulled up
> A white pickup truck

Even James sang the chorus to the Sara Evans song

A little pony-tailed girl
Grown up to be a woman
And she's gone in the blink of an eye

She left the suds in the bucket
And the clothes hanging out on the line*
* Recorded by Sara Evans, Nashville, Songwriters Billy Montana, Tammy Wagoner

Harlene joined in the verse about the beauty shop. Everyone had fun and they celebrated with a beer each.

"That was exceptionally good, Tori"

She thanked him and moved on to his departure.

"A car is picking me up around eight."

"From your hotel in town? When Stevie gets back we can drop you off, okay?"

"That'd be great. I'll call when I get home to see if there's news with the case. It's hard for me to leave any case without closure. I'd like to know if I was right all along about who the murderer is."

"It's understandable. I'll telephone daily with updates. So who do you think murdered Tilman now?" "I'll keep that to myself. No point influencing the investigation?" Okay, we won't be swayed, Tori, commented. "Your thoughts are very valuable though." "The suspects are Thomasina, Tug, Rory, Russ Jensen, Harlene, and from what Tug related, Cody or Jamie Chase."

"What? Why is Tug a suspect and Russ Jensen now?"

"Tug's in love with Harlene obviously. She's involved with Tilman. Getting him out of the way is expedient for him. He had access to the ice floe because it's his place and he also owns tugboats. Let me call Kip over. The band is on break now. James gestured to the guitarist, who walked over to the table."

"Kip, tell everyone what you told me about the faulty fireworks that injured Russ's dog."

Kip took a sip of beer and began explaining what he observed on the stage before the incident.

"Jensen was sometimes nervous before an important performance. He usually paced back and forth, chatted up with the band or went over lyrics. We talked first about chords then he mentioned the fireworks. He had noticed they were from Tilman Party Favors not the usual company, Zingers. He checked on speaker connections, then because he was the opening act, nodded to the band leader and touched Melody's ears, the signal for 'this is it.'"

"Was it the usual person setting off the fireworks?"

"Yeah, Bobby Nash—works for Stillwater Outdoor Entertainment. They oversee everything. During the explosion, Bobby was injured badly. I called for the ambulance waiting offstage. Stillwater arranges that just in case someone in the crowd or performers needs it. The extra excitement sometimes taxes body systems or there are the unexpected emergencies people have everywhere. Anyway they took Bobby to the hospital. I heard he's okay and has been released."

"I'm glad to hear it, though his resentment to Tilman might make him a suspect now," Tori said.

"But he had no opportunity being in the hospital during that time."

Just then Wood came back telling everyone that they made three arrests in Roarin Rory's.

"What! You found the murderer?" "No drug traffickers." "They were using purse exchange to supply opioids."

"Outside the entrance to the bar, I saw a friend, Purdy Overman…"

"Really?"

"I know–stage name. My friends' names sound like James Bond girls, funny. Anyway I asked for her help inside to watch out for any unusual activity at the bar–especially the purse hooks under it. I didn't want my uniform to scare anybody off. She's a good girl with an overactive sense of drama so she agreed enthusiastically."

"What happened?" "This lady came in and sat in the corner bar seat near Purdy's one. Judd, the bartender served her then grabbed the bar rag on the way to the register. Purdy said the woman had given him a one hundred dollar bill–unusual."

"Then Judd came around the bar, wiped the counter, underneath too. Purdy is no math whiz but noticed Judd only had ten dollars in his hand. He put it in her open purse along with a bottle of pills. Purdy pretended to not know where the purse hook was and knocked the woman's handbag on the floor spilling out everything—pills everywhere. I came in from outside when Purdy whistled loud enough. I stepped in and picked up a pill—opioid. I arrested everyone involved including Judd Stiles, the woman, Esmy (Esmeralda) Dawkins, Rory and even Purdy, who could get information from the others they wouldn't give to me." "Wouldn't they be suspicious of Purdy for whistling and knocking over the purse?"

Purdy is good at making up stories so I wasn't worried. I left them in the squad car and Purdy overheard Judd and Rory in a heated argument about something else—singer contracts. Judd threatened to expose Rory for making them sign over exclusive rights, without them knowing, unless he helped him get off drug charges. Rory hushed him and Esmy only stopped crying long enough to say "I need those pills for pain, I didn't know Judd got them from shaky sources".

Then she turned to face Purdy, "It's your fault. If you hadn't dumped my purse out…"

"When it looked like Purdy's exposure was imminent, I made an excuse about overcrowding the car and dragged her out. But I got good information from using her. She actually enjoyed it too. Rory was released immediately with impending fines or penalties. Esmy was too but Judd had to be locked up until a search of his residence and car could be initiated."

"Good job, James and Tori simultaneously agreed. It might not have anything to do with our murderer though the drug connection might end up being significant."

Griz, who seemed to appear out of the woodwork, walked over to Lieutenant James and said,

"It's Tilman's fault. He ignored laws, everyone's personal space, and only did what he wanted. I wouldn't be surprised if he supplied illegal drugs, too."

He grunted and stomped away into the back. On that angry note, the group paid up tabs and collected their belongings to get James to his hotel for returning to New York.

On the way, Tori asked James who he thought was most important to interview on Monday.

James replied, "They're all important. Do that in whatever order you want. The information learned will help either way. As he opened the car door at the hotel, James said cryptically,

There's someone else that's not on the list that is most likely our murderer."

Though Tori yelled out "Who?', James was gone.

※

Now that James had left, Tori felt the responsibilities more, but still competent. On her list for this Monday were finding Russ Jensen, talking to Chase about Harlene's tugboat (Tori looked forward to that for some reason), and getting information from Thomasina about the purse involved in the drug connection.

She phoned veterinary hospitals and found the dog, fitting Melody's description, and drove there only to find someone else found them first. It was Cody. The dog was now being released and the two guys were talking about what was needed for her convalescence. Melody came out walking but with the usual cumbersome cone around the neck. Cody knelt down gently on floor level patting her on the back. Russ smiled then turned to the receptionist for arranging payment. Tori took it in, noticing that Jensen obviously didn't have insurance or enough to pay. Cody jumped up and paid the bill, no questions asked. Russ shook his hand and thanked him. Tori, never liking to interrupt personal time, had to introduce herself now anyway. She patted the dog's nose first and said. "I'm Sargent Tori Calhoun, Mr. Jensen. May I ask a few questions now? It's about the murder of Taper Tilman on Friday. Do you know him or have heard what happened?"

"Nice to meet you, sir, or I guess ma'am is right. Everyone in the Nashville music business 'knows' him, usually as someone to avoid though. He's offered bogus contracts to musicians or singers. What did he die of? Choking on his own venom?"

"No, but he was murdered. Is that pleasing to you?"

"Can't even say I'm sorry though my mama would beat me upside the head for it."

"Where were you on Friday night after midnight?"

"Looking out for Melody. I slept outside."

"Out in the cold—no protection?" "I've got a Teton Sports sleeping bag with a nice mummy hood and draft tubes that are good to 180 C. The best $70 I've spent for camping out." "That's good. Can anyone verify you were there for the whole night?"

"Nope. No one was around. The vet's assistant inside might have seen me I guess." "I will check that. Couldn't you have eluded her and left for the river and killed Tilman?" "I could have but I didn't," Russ answered with emphasis.

Calhoun moved on.

"How about you now Cody? Sorry I didn't introduce myself to you earlier. Where were you Friday?" "Ruby's to start on that night. After that bar hopping–don't remember the order" "Went only to bars then, nowhere else?" "I did stop at Thomasina's for a Seven-up to counteract beer and because she's got this girl working Friday that gets the heart beating in my chest–you know what I mean."

"Sonia" Russ called out, sending a glance over to Cody.

Cody only nodded back. Tori wasn't surprised that two virile men would admire the girl though for one fleeting moment she wished she wasn't in police garb. Then remembering she was not a teenager and was a 27-year-old woman doing her investigative job, she asked Cody about familiarity with the victim.

Russ cut in immediately, "Cody's one of the ones burned by Tilman. I don't think we need to go into that but Cody wouldn't have killed him for it."

"Let Cody answer it then."

"I didn't choke Tilman, Officer Calhoun."

"Sargent is the title, for the record, okay. Did I say Tilman was choked?" "I think you did or I heard it somewhere."

"Stay available you two. Best to get Melody home now though." Tori reached down and scratched the dog's neck under the cone and smiled, "She's a beauty."

The three of them left and Tori next drove to Thomasina's place on the river. Her shop wasn't open now but Tori knocked on the side door Thomasina had used before.

"Hola," the woman inside greeted her. It wasn't Thomasina, but similar in looks.

"Sonia?"

"No she's off today. I'm Celita Salgado."

"What a beautiful name. Now Celita means heaven, right?"

"That's right. Are you here to shop now, because I closed the register? My mother isn't feeling very well."

"I'm sorry Thomasina's sick. Can I help? I'm a police Sargent, Tori Calhoun."

"Oh no thanks. She'll be fine—just worries excessively, since that man threatened to have us deported if we didn't stock his party favors or fireworks in the store. She wants me to finish school in the United States." "What man is that, Celita?"

"His name is Tilman. But I'm not sure if he's the one that just died. Our worries should be over."

"The murdered man had no authority in immigration though." "He threatened anyway to report bogus violations of conditions. Mom gets upset pretty easily about that. Me, I only laugh or get even by not filling his coffee thermos to the top." "Did he get refills often?" "Often enough,"

Thomasina heard the voices outside her bedroom and joined them.

"Hello again, Sargent Calhoun. What brings you over here now?"

"Investigating a purse sold here. It's evidence in a drug trafficking case we're working on. The woman bought a new one exactly like the old one she had used." "I remember it. It's not unusual for ladies to buy exact copies of a purse they like." "Do you have a merchant copy of the receipt?" "Somewhere I suppose. It's been a while. I'll look for it." She opened a vertical file box and found the needed receipt fairly quickly.

"Here you go."

She handed it over to Tori.

"Thanks, Thomasina and Celita. I appreciate it."

Tori turned the receipt over and left. The information that Tilman's thermoses were filled here was very interesting. Still nobody had located the one he used Friday night.

Jamie Chase was next on the list. Remembering that he might even be the murderer, Tori dispelled the image of him as handsome hunk and drove over to the repair shop. It didn't help that he walked outside to greet her holding an umbrella over her head to protect her from the rain that had begun. Tori thanked him when they were inside and took a few deep breaths.

"Jamie, how did you know I was arriving?"

"Surveillance cameras. Boats, especially speedy ones are attractive novelties to thieves. Glad you're not a thief, ma'am." The grin on his face threatened her resolve, but she recovered.

"Have you repaired Harlene's tugboat?"

"It is working now. It's pretty beat up outside."

"How's that?" "Scratches, pieces of wood embedded in the chrome strips around the outside."

"As law enforcement. I consider that evidence. Don't repair it or alter the finish. I'll have an officer pick it up later."

"I didn't destroy evidence drying out the engine, did I?"

Tori laughed out loud.

"No, if water in a boat was criminal evidence, the jails would be very full."

"For a policewoman, you've got one great sense of humor. I like that. Would you consider going out for dinner. I'm not a candlelight or caviar type–just sandwiches and beer."

"I'm not allowed to accept or be bribed." "It's not a bribe, sincerely."

From experience, Tori knew being in uniform had two results—occasionally idealizing the person inside or usually resentment and stereotyping of the wearer. Instinct told her Jamie's response wasn't either, so she only smiled, all the way trying to think of a way to get him her phone number. Instead she asked one important question.

"Where is your tugboat- meaning the privately owned one?"

"Still think I whacked the guy?"

"He was the one behind the record deal going sour and associated ills."

"Oh well, that makes me despise him, not kill him. Doing that I'd lose God's respect and my own too."

Tori thought she didn't need more to like about him now, only it was what it was.

He stood and walked over to the window facing the river. Suddenly her body heat rose as their moist lips locked in intense need and abandon. His hands on her face tenderly guided the kiss over and over until she felt fierce desire in every inch of their bare skins. If heaven is anywhere… Tori thought, then looked up and saw fully clothed Jamie just standing there. She instinctively consulted her wristwatch to see how much time had elapsed while imagination had taken over her senses. She'd checked the time when Chase got up, making a mental note to deduct one minute from her time sheet later. Couldn't have the department paying for imagined sex dreams on the job, right? Also hoping Jamie was not telepathically gifted she continued asking. "Your tugboat is where?"

"I don't own one. Haven't used one for a month but I usually take a rental. Can't remember which one. Let's go outside and check." Tori needed the fresh air to stop thinking of sex so she nodded.

Chase put on a jacket and gloves, while Tori got out hers. Obviously the tugs were tarped but Jamie unhooked the various tie-downs to reveal them.

"I remember now—the orange one there." Tori wasn't interested in a boat used in the past, only on Friday night. Having learned from Lieutenant James, she studied everything and found nothing very unusual but recorded the boat numbers in her notebook. When she finished, Chase asked, "Do you give out your phone number or only from the precinct?"

'Here's my opportunity' thought Calhoun. She handed him the usual business card with her cell number written on it. "Telephone the department if you find or remember anything unusual that's related to Tilman or the incident at Tug's"

She deliberately omitted mention of phoning her personally but Jamie grinned on looking at the card, though he used 'Sargent' instead of 'Tori' when saying goodbye as she left. That helped her remember her job and that he was still a viable murder suspect.

Not looking forward to the next visit of the hospitalized girl injured in Cody's accident, she took one deep breath and drove to Nashville Memorial Hospital. Traffic was very heavy so she used the flashing lights but not the siren. No use frightening everyone, she thought.

Navigating around almost stopped cars she got glimpses of local attractions, First, the Bicentennial Capitol State Park and the carillon bells in its Court of Three Stars were playing the old favorite, Tennessee Waltz. Ryman Auditorium was next, only allegedly cursed, reporting hauntings from Hank Williams Senior. Closer in a downtown neighborhood was Printer's Alley where someone who was murdered is frequently seen with his dog. That made her think of Russ Jensen and Melody. She had to be impartial and pragmatic though. Jensen's motive for murdering Tilman was strong. Tilman's irresponsible fireworks manufacturing had hurt the most important thing in Russ's life.

Next was the Johnny Cash Museum directional sign. She'd never been there but it housed more memorabilia than even the Grammy Museum in LA. The police scanner was on now but she hummed "Ring of Fire" as she steered on past the exit. For the "it goes down, down down" part she sang, "It goes down down town instead. After exiting, access to the hospital was easy. On the driveway, valet parking was available but squad cars had in front of the building privileges. At the desk inside too, usual regulations were waived and a nurse escorted her quickly to the girl's hospital room. Tori automatically checked the outside clipboard to be sure the name matched. Harlene had supplied the girl's name, Callie Thorpe, and it was the same on the hospital record. Harlene had been reluctant to give her that information at first since Cody's alleged negligence caused the injury to the girl, but she must have decided talking to the girl might eventually help him."

Tori knocked then entered without waiting for a reply the way doctors often do. Surprisingly, Callie was not in bed but standing over by the window. She spoke first, "Oh, you're not the discharge nurse, only the police. I've given enough statements, ma'am. I want to go home and see my horse."

"How great to have a horse. I thought injuries to your back prevented riding though. I'm Sargent Tori Calhoun, Callie. You can use Tori, if police titles are uncomfortable to use."

Callie ignored the name question entirely saying, "It's true. I can't ride yet. I just want to brush Sadie." She climbed back in the hospital bed. It looked awkward, but then surgery on back vertebrae had a very long healing time. The nurse finally spoke up, "Callie, stay in bed. You don't want to irritate or re-injure the back," The monitor on Cora's belt (nurse's name) beeped once and she excused herself to investigate another patient's needs. Callie's expression changed from bored to almost furious anger. "Cora tells my folks everything I do, then they threaten to take Sadie away from me. They've been doing that since I got here. It's unfair." The floodgates opened and she sobbed uncontrollably.

Tori was not a mother yet but once again instinct ruled. She found a tissue for Callie and offered a hug, which was reciprocated immediately. "I'm so sorry all this happened to you because of an irresponsible young guy." Callie looked up and stared, then sobbed even more using her hands to gesture 'no'. "What is upsetting about what I just said?"

"I know all that stuff the news reported on that guy. I even know his name is Cody Sted, but he didn't cause it. It was the older man in the driver's seat that day. He visited my parents and paid hospital expenses if I stuck to the story that Cody drove. What was I supposed to do?"

She sobbed even harder.

"They're going to be furious with me but I can't stand being secretive or lying. I think that's interfering with my fast healing, too."

"Callie, I wish I could make it all better. Maybe telling the truth is cathartic."

"What does it mean, cathartic?"

"Something that releases build-up of extreme emotional tension. It's like a purge for the soul."

"Sounds like what I need. I'm only an eleven year old. Too much angst isn't good."

"Wow, nice knowing that word."

"It's from a Jason Aldean song. I like him."

"Now, who doesn't?"

"Callie, would it be all right if I asked you to positively identify the driver from this photo?"

"Okay, yeah, all right. I'm doomed anyway."

"No you're not. I'll assure your parents of the need for not keeping it inside. And I'm not disappearing either. If anything bad occurs, telephone me. Here's my number. I'll see that they don't take Sadie ever too. Unless the horse gets too old, that is. What age is she?"

"She's only four, no glue factory anywhere in the future. Thanks, Tori."

※

Tori gently held the newspaper photo of Tilman's image to Callie's outstretched hand.

"Yep, No doubt that's the face I saw sitting in the driver's seat of the car that hit the bike and of course, me."

Callie turned her head into the pillow as if to hide from the memory.

"I'm so sorry that happened to you, but the memory fades, given time. Now you've got brushing Sadie to look forward to." She sat up and grinned brightly. "I just know I'll feel better when home and I can see her."

"Callie, I understand. I had a pony named Maybelle when I was nine. I loved her." She smiled looking out of the window remembering. She asked, "Callie does anyone other than your own parents know of Tilman's switch?"

"Only Cody's mother, Harlene. She visited me—a nice lady. I got a medallion for Sadie's bridle as a gift from her; only the nurses took that away. They thought I might swallow it, I guess, or it had germs. Honestly, I might act crazy like normal teenagers but I'm not stupid. Anyway, Cody's mom was upset because she did not believe that he did it. I had to tell her the fact that he didn't. I had to lie to my folks when they found out she had been here. I can't keep secrets very well."

"Thanks, Callie. When was this visit?" "IT was Wednesday of last week, if I remember. It's hard to keep track in the hospital, but I get ice cream on Wednesdays and they brought that right after I said goodbye to her." Tori thanked the girl and said goodbye as the nurse came in to take usual blood pressure readings. She hoped the conversation hadn't caused it to be unusually high. It wasn't. She wasn't worried very much. Callie's strong heart would handle it. It was worth finding out about Harlene. *So Harlene knew of the driver switch and must have been furious about it–Enough to kill Tilman even, a very strong motive.* Next thing was getting the report on Harlene's tugboat damage for evidence. Detectives had to be impartial, only personally she hoped Harlene was innocent. She liked her.

Back in the police station, she visited the lab immediately for news.

Earl was standing, hand on hips, looking in a culture dish inserted in a microscope.

"Find anything, Earl?" she asked.

He looked up from his work and nodded affirmatively.

"Striations in wood are distinctive indicators of type. These I found are exact matches to scaffolding wood used in Tug's ice floe."

"That's good. Where are they from?"

"Chase's Rental tugboat." He said emphatically without inflection.

"No, it's from the one you had towed."

"Harlene's tugboat?" "I don't know. We assign numbers not ownership to eliminate prejudice in findings. I'll cross-reference that for you Sargent."

Tori thought it was good the boat wasn't one of Jamie Chase's, though it didn't look good for Harlene.

"Here it is. The tugboat belongs to one Harlene Sted."

Using her to-do list for distraction from inevitable Harlene arrest later in the day she checked it over:

Visit Tilman's wife

Question vet assistant about Russ Jensen's overnight there

Find witnesses to Friday night disturbance

Thermos bottle?

Not exactly sure how to proceed determining who filled up the thermos, she only knew the drugs found in it were important. It showed premeditation. If Harlene put the coffee in, that made the case open and shut for her. Taking one thing at a time, she drove to Gaybelle Tilman's in Gulch.

Her apartment faced east on the secluded side street near the main drag through town. Purple flowers and bordering of daffodils were evidence of the sun's morning light on them. She wondered if an outside service maintained the immaculate garden. From Wick's description, his mother couldn't manage that.

Tori pushed the intercom and announced her name. The buzzer unlocked the door and Mrs. Tilman opened it the rest of the way for her. Though Calhoun expected pajamas and slippers, the woman was in cowboy boots, a turquoise top and neat jeans—So much for bedridden status.

"Good afternoon." Tori greeted.

"Well, howdy now Sargent. I'm Gaybelle, skipping the Tilman, as I dropped that the way he dropped me." "Sorry that happened. I only have a few questions. Did you ever know Taper to do drugs?" "I sometimes thought he took a meanness drug, though I can't say about others."

"Oh, I see." Tori said aloud but thought two things. Despite her pulled together outfit there was no way the diminutive woman had enough strength to choke and overpower the victim. And, though Gaybelle claimed no knowledge of Taper's activities, Tori believed she knew more about a lot of things than saying now.

"Did your son, Wick, work in the garden? It looks great." Change of subject sometimes helped in her experience.

"No, it's a service. Wick picked the flowers, though. He's a good son, even with a philandering father."

Back to that, Tori tried again.

"If you don't mind, what financial provisions have been made for you and your boy?"

"If it had been up to my husband, former mind you, we'd have nothing, though the courts decided on a nice tidy sum for both of us to live on if he died. For some reason, Taper never changed the will and the whole worth of his business passes to us. Wick could use that."

"What exactly does he do?"

"He's a header."

"What's that now?" "Bulldoggers in steer wrestling come in two forms. The header, using the first rope over head or horns, the heeler, using a second rope to catch the calf's legs." "So it's rodeo stuff?"

"Yeah, work is slow for now though." "Thanks for the information, Gaybelle. Is there anything I can do for you?" "Outside of warm up the weather, no, there's nothing." "I may have further questions later on. I'll keep you informed of developments and temperature."

She chuckled and waved once, going toward the door.

"Sargent, I'm not afraid of questions. Just know, though, if I was gonna kill Taper, I'd have done it long before now."

Tori braced herself for the next task—arresting Harlene. She telephoned headquarters to have two "uniforms" meet her at Raging Ruby's where Harlene was likely to be this afternoon, She needed the back up as Cody and Griz might fight the arrest.

MURDER ON THE ICE FLOE IN NASHVILLE

Tori had a heart though and timed the arrest for when the bar wasn't very full. She met the officers' patrol car outside and they went in together,

Harlene was washing Mason jar glasses in the sink and dropped one seeing the police enter. Thinking they were there for Cody she gestured to Griz then spoke up, "What can I do for you officers?"

Tori answered, "I'm sorry but we have to arrest you for Taper Tilman's murder. There's evidence your tugboat destroyed the ice floe." Tori pulled out the faded photo of the young girl and said, "This was found in Taper's pocket. Our experts found sufficient points of match with a photo of you to conclude she's a relative. We think Tilman was using that to blackmail you."

"She is my daughter, only Taper had lots of money. I don't. Why would he extort me?"

"Do you deny he was using your daughter inappropriately?" "No, I can't. He somehow obtained indecent pictures of her, threatening exposure if I didn't go along with his demands." Harlene started sobbing. Immediately Tug, sitting at the bar, jumped up and put his hand on her shoulder, saying, "Admittedly it's a motive for damaging the ice floe Tilman was on, but I did that. I used her tugboat." Calhoun responded, "Did you now? Or are you willing to commit perjury being gallant?" "Tug, don't do it." Harlene said, "I appreciate your intent, that's not necessary though." She touched Tug's arm tenderly.

Just then Griz and Cody walked in closer having heard that the police were intent on arrest. Cody's face seemed inscrutable but his hands were clenched in tight fisted form. Griz boldly said, "NO.

It don't add up. Harlene is no killer. Me, maybe, arrest me instead. If all you have is motive, I've got it too."

Tori only nodded and turned to Cody, "I suppose you want to volunteer being arrested instead, too? Though it's a credit to Harlene's personality, there is another strong motive. Cody, did you know that Callie's injuries were actually caused by Tilman's driving error, not yours?" Now, Cody looked stricken and even genuinely surprised.

"I didn't–first I heard of it."

"Well, okay, but your mother did. She must have been furious at Taper–probably enough to kill since he showed no consideration to your troubles from it. I did consider you as suspect though I checked out the bars and enough people remembered you there at the time of the murder."

"Glad of an alibi, but my mother didn't do it. You're making a mistake in arresting her."

Griz nodded his head too and stood firmly near Harlene.

At the corner table a group of woman were finishing up a late lunch. They were not drinking and stopped talking about recipes for desserts when they heard the police use the word murder. One middle-aged woman got up from the table and strode hesitantly to Calhoun, who turned toward her.

"My name's Patty Jo Foster, ma'am. I don't intend to butt in. though if it helps this woman, owner of the establishment, I need to do it. God knows all it takes is for a few good men or women to do nothing... I forget the rest of that expression...anyway I was on the riverbank on Friday night when she was on the tugboat." Calhoun was now very interested.

"I'll need your personal information for the report later, Miss Foster, but tell what you saw now."

"It's Mrs.–I left Roarin Rory's with my husband, Ian. He drinks on the weekends and sometimes I have to go get him out of there, like on Saturdays especially, so we can make it to church on Sunday morning."

"MRS. Foster, the murder was on Friday night. Are you sure about seeing Harlene on Friday night now?"

"O yes absolutely. Ian and I went out on Friday too. I don't know what he does at the bar–well drinks of course–but it's not the other woman thing so I'm grateful for that..."

Tori's inclination was to hurry her along in the story but knew from experience you had to let these types of hypertensive women talk it out or they left things out...

"I heard noise out on the river. I saw this lady (gesturing toward Harlene) ramming into the fishing frame several times and yelling."

Harlene's heart sank inside. If the police had an actual eyewitness, she felt the jail cell doors closing and locking her in interminably. Cody felt elation, not causing the girl's injuries earlier, but the situation facing his mother erased that high. If he was bipolar, it couldn't be worse experiencing the opposite emotions.

Patty Jo continued on, "Ian was leaning on me so we walked very slowly on the bank. The noise of crunching ice and wood was hard to avoid…"

"And then?" Calhoun said.

"Ian was getting heavy to hold and there was a bench on the path so I set him there, looking up across the river. There were three vehicles parked in Tug's lot facing the River. Then the woman on the tugboat throttled the engine down and quit ramming the ice. The man fishing yelled something in the quiet and she left immediately, heading toward this bar. Ian stood up and the fresh air revived him enough to walk himself. We headed for the car and got in to leave."

Calhoun asked, "Can you verify that the man fishing was alive when the tugboat left the ice floe?"

"Yes I can. The man's slurred speech reminded me of Ian knee deep in drinking nights. There were times I thought he was dead, too, when he closed his eyes. I couldn't see that man's eyes though obviously the shouting indicates he was alive."

"Thanks for the information, Patty Jo. I have two more questions now, and then you can expect to testify about this in the preliminary hearing. Harlene may face attempted murder charges."

"Ask me officer, I'll try to answer it."

"Was it usual for you two to be out that late on weekends?"

"For Ian, yes. I went to enjoy a performer who rarely appears publicly, but so good."

"Who was it?" "Jamie Chase"

Tori had to admit personally feeling relieved, but still annoyed that Jamie hadn't told her he had an alibi for that Friday night.

"Continuing, Tori asked, Do you remember anything about the three vehicles parked over at Tug's?"

"Sure I do. A red sports car in the corner of the lot."

Cody answered,

"That's Taper's car."

"A brown Toyota truck, and an orange Kubota tractor."

Tug spoke up, "That's my Kubota for assisting boaters."

Nobody could identify the brown truck.

"I don't suppose the plate number was clear from that distance, Patty?"

"Oh you're wrong. It was a vanity plate–R-O-D-E-O"

Back at headquarters, Tori telephoned Lieutenant James now in New York. Still not sure of the decision to let Harlene free on her own recognizance, she instructed one officer to stay and follow her movements. If she bolted or tried leaving the bar, he was told to detain her unless she was going home for the night.

James answered the phone immediately on second ring.

"Tori, how's things there?"

"Hi, Eli, I hope you're free now. I have accumulated some problems but I solved others."

"That's good. I should say. Bitsy and I are travelling to Nashville tomorrow. She's a substantial shareholder of Bank of America based there and wants to vote at the meeting in person. The Schwartz Foundation, her husband's legacy, is paying for expenses."

"Hallelujah! That is great news. Can I meet you at the airport for transport here?"

"Bitsy's personal secretary is travelling with us and has arranged our limo. It'll swing by headquarters and drop me off, but thanks for the offer. What are the new developments there?" "Well, Harlene did use her tugboat to ram the scaffolding at Tug', but a witness that night verifies Tilman was alive when she left the fishing area. Russ Jensen's alibi, sleeping outside the vet's, has not been verified, though. Cody's in the clear for that night." She told him about Callie and the information that Tilman's driving injured her, not Cody's.

"It's a possible motive for the parents, definitely for Cody. Unless someone was with him the whole time, he could have slipped out. Any other news?" "There is more. It can wait until you're here in Nashville."

"Okay, that's fine," James responded.

"Now do you still think your instinct is pointing to the murderer? Tori asked."

MURDER ON THE ICE FLOE IN NASHVILLE

"I believe neither Thomasina or Harlene is strong enough to overpower Tilman to choke him. I considered Jamie Chase but why would he wait years to carry out revenge now? From what you said about Tilman's wife, she's not strong enough either. Russ Jensen's motive is strong though I believe he's not a killer. Was the thermos Tilman drank from ever found?" "It's odd. It wasn't. Is that important?" Tori asked.

"It didn't just disappear. The drug was in there and who filled it could be an important clue. Someone must have removed it. It didn't sink to the river bottom. They dragged it." James continued, "I've got a theory–tell you tomorrow. I need to pack now. Good work so far, Tori. I knew you'd do a bang up job. Tomorrow then." "Thanks, James. Have a safe trip." Tori rechecked with forensics about the thermos but they'd never found any evidence of it. The murderer must have retrieved it.

James and Bitsy enjoyed first class on the flight from New York, though he would have rather liked getting her luggage down from the overhead himself. He liked the opportunity to stretch up after sitting uncomfortably for so long. As usual, he thanked the pilot and flight crew and they headed to ground transportation. Rob, Bitsy's former driver, now personal secretary caught up with them then picked up the limo outside.

A gentle rain during the night gave way to patches of blue in the sky and crisp fresh air. Rob had anticipated their hunger and ordered waffle eggs and bacon from the Berry Field Bistro inside. The limo included a bar, energy drinks and water, now enough food to last the trip into downtown.

Promising to meet Bitsy for dinner in Raging Ruby's, James got out at the police station, finding Sargent Calhoun inside. Over coffee they discussed recent developments. James seemed especially interested in the Toyota truck Patty Jo Foster noticed in Tug's parking lot that Friday night.

"When did she see it that night/morning?"

"It was around Rory's usual closing time: 2:00 am."

"Medical examiner concluded time of death at 2:30."

James looked very thoughtful, but said, "Tori, I think we need to visit Tug again."

"He wasn't even there then, though."

"It's for another reason. I'll explain at Tug's. Is there a car available?"

"James you should know there's always a squad car queued up to use."

"Different in New York, I often have to use my Cadillac for work."

"Okay I suppose that's true. I'll intercom Stevie for a car now though."

Calhoun got the necessary transportation and said, "Let's go."

No sirens necessary, they sped over to Tug's. The river was slightly higher from the rain but nowhere flooded.

"James, are you thinking Tug killed Tilman or something else?"

"No, something else. Tug wouldn't risk incarceration to jeopardize a budding relationship with Harlene. Tug knows something though. Just a hunch."

Tug met them at the office door, looking innocent but still wary of the reason for the police visit now. He welcomed them in but didn't offer seats or coffee. Sensing the trouble to come, he slumped on the closest chair and looked up at them.

James could look imposing and formidable standing tall taking a certain stance and he did so now. He spoke firmly, "Tug, where is the thermos?"

Tug answered very quickly, "Oh do you want coffee?" James scowled and said in a deep voice, "You know what thermos I mean."

Tug rose, sighing, and went out to the kitchen. Tori and James heard the squeaky oven door open and close. He returned with a green Stanley Thermos with raised letters on the outside.

"I found it floating, sort of stuck, under the dock. It could be anybody's…his voice trailed off."

"But it's not, Tug." James took it from Tug and examined the insignia and words written on it. The rodeo raised lettering etched on the side was all he needed.

"It was in the oven?" Tori asked.

"Yeah, now I'm sorry I hid it. I don't use the oven though; I cook everything in the microwave. I'm no gourmet."

Tori laughed a little inside, remembering Tug's "buffet" for them earlier. More important to the investigation now, she asked, "Did you wash it?"

"No. I thought I'd give it back the next day, but there were forensic police outside and you were in here. Ah hell, I knew what the thermos meant. Wick did his daddy in. I didn't want to face it. He stopped over after rodeos and a few beers later, he talked about his grandparent, and how he wished they were still here now. Once he hinted that his father caused their deaths. In Tilman's eyes, Wick was nobody to be proud of. That had to hurt. Rodeo success stroked his ego though deep down he was one troubled kid. I should have helped him more."

"Tug, don't fret over it. Some kinds of trouble have no easy fix."

Tori asked, "James how did you even know what to look for; the thermos, Wick's involvement, all of it?"

"My first thought was no woman had enough strength to bring down Tilman for choking. He would've fought back. Tug, here, might have wanted to eliminate Tilman out of love for Harlene, Strong enough motive, but no opportunity. That leaves us Russ Jensen, Cody and Jamie. Rory was occupied at the bar. Jensen would not have abandoned Melody, and Cody was seen elsewhere. Wick's comment over at Tug's got me thinking though. He brought up strangulation there and it wasn't yet revealed as cause of death. Then later he offered replacing the pedal boat, which definitely wasn't public knowledge and forensics hadn't found the ruins of that. When I asked Tug about it, he said that he did not tell Wick about either."

Now that Wick was the most likely of culprits, Tori relaxed that Jamie was out of the running for murderer. Not that she believed he could have committed it anyway,

She asked, "What implicated Wick most?"

"His hands and smell. That was first. When he was here at Tug's, his hands were cut up and even swollen. His body smell had faint remnants of river scum. Even the shower can't remove the lingering odor. Your info from Patty Jo Foster put his truck on the river at the scene of the crime. His rodeo expertise in roping steer made it plausible he was capable of roping even a big man. I just guessed that Tug found the thermos. The forensic police on that day also reported that Wick viewed the debris they found and seemed to be searching for something."

"The lab needs to check it inside for drugs but it doesn't look good for Wick. Tug, spoliation of evidence, or withholding it is considered a felony in most states. However, the thermos was found on your property, making it *ipso facto* yours, even if only temporarily. So probably no charges." "Probably isn't a certainty," Tug mused out loud.

"Don't worry about it. It'll be okay. We've got to go over to the lab. If all goes as expected we'll celebrate the case being over at Raging Ruby's later on. You should come."

"If celebrating is at Wick's expense, I doubt I can manage it. I will try."

"For Harlene's sake, you should. She escaped arrest, after all."

"True."

After the lab examination confirmed the presence of opioid drugs in bottom of the thermos, the police chief decided evidence was sufficient for arresting Wick Tilman.

Bitsy's shopping trip took hours. The record shop was first. She got Kenny Rogers albums for everyone. His passing on caused fans to buy them just to hear that wonderful voice again. She'd heard it on the radio that he was the first country musician to achieve status in two genres, country and pop fame.

Next was Dillard's for supplementary clothing and cosmetics not allowed in carry-on baggage on the plane. An important stop for something for James took a while but she found it worth it. For souvenirs she went to Nashville Limited, Turnip Truck Urban Fare for food and the Goo Goo Shop for the famous candy.

Going back to headquarters, James noticed the steep slopes alongside that part of the Cumberland River.

"Hard to launch boats over there." he gestured to Tori.

"True, though climbing sport is popular."

"This area is a sportsman's ideal paradise. Very lovely."

"We like it. Thanks for saying that."

"If I know Bitsy, there's a shopping trip following the meeting and free catered lunch. She often likes to gift favorite people, (and fortunately that's me) while traveling to interesting places."

MURDER ON THE ICE FLOE IN NASHVILLE

"Several great stores are in Nashville. Ernest Tubb Record Shop is famous, for superior boots, there's Nashville Boot Company."

"Speaking of boots," James held up one foot, "I got these from Bitsy in New York. They're inspired by one Toby Keith song, 'The Baddest Boots in the Boulevard' from his Shocking Y'all album."

"Handmade genuine fine horned back kick with its seven row stitch."

"They're great, James."

"All I need is a cowboy hat to fit in this crazy town."

Tori looked very thoughtful, picturing him as the eminent detective he was famous for, turned cowboy. She laughed inside.

Waiting for the warrant to arrest Wick, James spent the time talking with officers Stevie and Wood in headquarters. Stevie had looked up James' bio and was eager for more details.

"Tell us about your famous solvings."

"Well I just did my job the way you two do."

That only made Stevie more interested.

"Were most of them involving drugs, poisons?"

It was difficult for James to ignore her eager questions and remain humble, though he tried.

"In Manhattan, following blowfish poisoning, a trail of offshore money laundering emerged leading to solving it. A case of gangsters avoiding recognition using plastic surgery also involved drug traffickers using song lyrics to pass on locations for buying them."
"How did it do that?"

"They used hotel room numbers. One example is the Beach Boys '409'"

"The case I call The Numbered Cups Mystery involved poisoning when cups, using numbers for identification for guests, got switched causing a writer's death,"

"I have to say, though, killing someone, no matter how horrible they were, is not right. I'm sure you've heard of dogged detectives. It's not personal, but focus on finding a murderer has to be that way."

"Good advice in that, Lieutenant James. Thanks."

The clerk informed them that the warrant was ready. James stood up and said, "I hope you two will join us and everyone at Ruby's for dinner, having been involved in this case early on. We may need you this afternoon, too."

"We're on call. We'll be there for dinner, too, especially if someone else pays." "It's on Bitsy. She's a very generous person. I'm lucky to have met her in Manhattan."

"I'm happy for you. Catch you later on, Lieutenant."

James picked open the lock on the front door, and being very cautious, Tori with gun out, they entered Wick's apartment. After checking the rooms to be sure no one was still there, they searched for clues that might indicate where he'd gone. For a man, the place was neat, except for the desk. A stack of bills lay near the computer. James grabbed the one on top and read the banner–Cabella's–it was for new climbing gear.

"Hmm," Tori mused out loud. "I pushed the back button on the computer. It's the Cumberland Bluffs website and application for the gate code."

"What is Cumberland Bluffs?"

"One of the venues to rock climb in our area. We passed it on our way to headquarters remember? You commented on the steep slopes over the river."

"James, here's a note addressed to 'Mom'"

"Open it."

"It says, *'I'm sorry it came to this, mom. I love you'*. That's all."

"Okay, in that case, we better get a move on. If I'm right, Wick's life is in danger."

"Well I agree."

"Wick is planning on ending his life on that mountain. We'll need climbing gear."

"Thomasina's has that."

"Let's go now."

Outside, a neighbor was bringing in his trashcan. James hurriedly asked, "Did you see this guy leave earlier?" "Yep–half hour ago."

"What was he wearing?"

"Who is asking?"

James explained they were detectives from the police.

"Okay, orange tassel cap and red parka, carrying an ice axe and spiky things."

"Thanks"

Tori called ahead to Thomasina's and requested ice picks and flexible crampons for their boots. Not surprising, she had everything they needed ready. What was a surprise, though, Jamie Chase was inside too.

He greeted them at the front and said. "It looks like you folks are going mountain climbing. I don't want to interfere with police business but I'm an experienced climber and guide—worked for the Climbers Coalition at Cumberland Bluffs for six months."

"That's where we're headed now. Care to join our expedition?"

"Absolutely," Jamie said, looking one admiring glance toward Tori. "Most important gear is first, helmet, then a pair of gloves and rope harness if rappelling's needed. The crampons you have are good, but the ice pick axes aren't useful. The bluff is limestone and not very resilient or soft even. Bring them anyway. They're useful for balance up steep slopes."

Tori asked, "Isn't rappelling dangerous?"

"It sure is. A woman fell fifty feet, free fall. Eventually landing on water's edge. A riverboat took her to Clarksville Marina and immediately Life Flight picked her up. It's not recommended for the inexperienced climber. I can get you safely up the 80 feet of most of the routes. May I ask why you're going?"

"A murder suspect is headed there."

"Okay, you're going to make an arrest on the mountain?"

"It's more than that, Jamie. Wick Tilman left a suicide note."

"Oh, Tilman's son, and you think he's a jumper then?"

"We're trying to stop it. One reason that I pursue criminals is that I don't believe anyone has the right to kill, no matter how despicable the victim. My faith and convictions include not letting others take their own life, if you can prevent that either."

Stevie and Wood in the car ahead of Jamie's truck cut the sirens immediately as they turned off into the parking lot.

"That's good." James stated. "I've been on rooftops with a nervous jumper. Usually police cars and sirens make it worse."

"What is your plan for this, Lieutenant?" Jamie asked, "I'm just a ride along now."

"No your guiding's important. We've got to survive ultimately too. We're only three ordinary rock climbers on an outing. That's what we want to exude. You're helping there, though if you spot that orange tassel cap, make note of the location. Until then, he could be anywhere."

They put on gear at the gate, using the given code for unlocking it. Jamie helped out with the crampons and offered advice. "Never look down at where you've been. Focus on next step up. It'll be fine."

"Sounds good for life too."

They started the ascent.

They set out following Jamie's lead and it was not too steep because the route he'd picked for them didn't go straight up the slope. After a few halting steps. James got a rhythm going but Tori took to it easily, catching up to Jamie above her.

She heard his strong lyrical voice above her.

> "It was only a mountain
> Nothing but a big ol' rock
> Only a mountain
> It ain't hard if you don't stop
> You just take a little step
> A right then a left
> A couple million more
> Who's counting?
> Hell it's only a mountain"*

- Written by Dierks Bentley, Luke Dick, Jon Randall and Natalie Hemby, UMG recording 2019 Dierks Bentley

Suddenly James' jacket got hooked on a tall bramble and though he knew better, he looked down for loosening it. When he freed it he looked up and Tori and their guide were not there—Nowhere in sight! Not the type to panic, James searched again near a large boulder on his right. There it was, the orange cap Wick was wearing. Apparently Tori had seen it too and was perched on the rock near the precipice and the suspect. James scurried there faster than he thought possible.

Wick spoke to them. "This is a public place, I understand, but I want to be alone now."

James spoke back first, "Wick, your mother needs you now. Won't you come down?"

"Oh, you're the police guy. I remember now. My mother's fine. I checked on her yesterday. What do you want of me?"

"We know you killed your father in the ice fishing arena. He wasn't a very good dad, was he?"

"Hell no, more of a curse. Yeah I did the deed. I did everyone a favor. I know about Russ Jensen's dog, Cody's accident and Harlene's troubles he caused even. I couldn't take it anymore."

"He's responsible for killing my grandparents too. I found the apple butter jars and antimony used in fireworks in the garage when he was out sowing wild oats with an employee. She wasn't important to him, like I wasn't, just somebody he could use to get "it" when he wanted. He killed them, his own parents, to get control of the family business. My name, Wick is for candles, but his name should be "Wicked". That's the name he deserved."

James knew the signs of extreme distress from Wick's body language. He got up suddenly and took a step toward the edge of the boulder. The others breathed in sharply in unison. James just kept on talking, "You know if you jump a worst thing might even happen."

"What, I'll die?" How is that not worse? Nobody's gonna miss me.

"No, Wick, you might survive it ending up paralyzed forever or brain impaired. A fall from 50 feet here isn't likely to kill you."

"Yeah? How do you know it? How do you figure?"

"In the spring, a woman fell that distance, had to be Life-Flighted with severe injuries. Think of your mother. Do you really want her changing your diapers or feeding baby food the rest of your life?"

That did it. Wick backed off from the edge. Wick's face, though, was drained of normal color and his breathing was rapid. James gestured to Tori to offer comfort to him. She gently laid a hand on his arm. He seemed to relax.

James took the opportunity to signal administration using preset code with the important message, "Send the copter."

The risk travelling down the mountain with Wick's emotional state was more than necessary. James had time to prepare him for the rescue too. In less than four minutes the rope ladder for them dropped down from the helicopter beating above everyone. Wick going first, they ascended to the cabin. Wick seemed to actually enjoy using the ladder. You don't get far in rodeo without an adventurous spirit.

"Don't everybody sit on the same side. That makes it hard to balance. I'm Captain Bill Smith, y'all. Which one is Lieutenant James?"

"That is me," James said climbing inside the chopper. "Mighty grateful for the ride."

"Sure thing. Though I can only take three people at one time."

Tori, with her firearm hidden, took a seat next to Wick.

Jamie, waiting on the rope, heard that and called to James. "I'll go down the mountain way. I've gotta pick up my truck anyway. Godspeed."

Captain Bill waited till Jamie was free of the rope and released the hover hold. He yelled, "All set now y'all? Headed for the Metro Heliport, unless you change it."

James answered, "No change needed. Thanks."

James noted Wick's interest in how the helicopter remained in hover position over the heliport now. The pilot found a fixed spot outside of the cockpit and tracked how the copter moved relative to that point. Easing back on the cyclic stick, forward motion stopped. Adjusting the collective, an interior lever for making changes in pitch, then twisting the throttle the helicopter remained in place. The ground level of the heliport made for easy exiting. Since the noise was deafening, hand gestures or body language replaced talking until the copter lifted upward and was seen as only a faint bright spot in the sky. Most of the workers inside had come out to see the unusual sight. Wick seemed unnerved by that and James moved in toward him to reassure him.

Two cars, actually one limo and an Uber taxi pulled into the now crowded parking lot. James continued reassuring Wick.

"Best shot is a good criminal lawyer to get you through this. You're a grown man and it'll be okay. The taxi reached the pair first with dozens of police readying in case of attempted escape of the murderer, however the Uber driver only released the passenger and moved on."

It was Gaybelle and one distinguished looking older man.

"Wick, this is Richard Ramsey, a fine lawyer, to help you."

The police, uncomfortable with an unsecured alleged murderer, stepped in quickly and handcuffed Wick, in front of Tori and James for witnessing there was no brutality. They led him inside.

"I've got your back son. This is only temporary," Gaybelle called out loudly.

The gawkers dispersed inside and James stretched to his considerable height, saying now, "He's going to need psychiatric evaluation now before sentencing. It's not a case of either justifiable homicide or cold-blooded murder. The courts will sort it out eventually. If it turns out to be guilt from insanity, the medical profession will decide on his fate. We've done everything we can now on our end. Trusting in the future fair outcome is not only our job but also it's our release. Thanks to everyone involved. Let's enjoy Ruby's, free from guilt or worry."

Just then the limo pulled up in front of James and he took it as a good sign that normal was restored and motioned to Bitsy inside. The backseat door swung open and he slid in comfortably beside her. Touching her hand gently and smiling, he added. "Glad you didn't 'drop' from 'shopping' dear."

"Likewise, Eli, glad you didn't 'drop' off that mountain."

Though Bitsy's intuition wasn't surprising, James wondered.

"You know about that?"

"It was on the news. I turned on the television to catch Oprah Winfrey (she's from Nashville) and there you were–on a boulder halfway up the steep slopes. Fortunately the news also covered the helicopter rescue."

"I see from the tons of packages shopping worked out."

He peeked in the bags however they were all wrapped in tissue and bows.

"I guess I have to wait for what's inside the packages."

"That's right, the car's almost to Ruby's now anyway."

Griz came out to meet them. He'd never seen a limousine up close enough to see inside before. His face in a big smile, he tried the door only to find it wouldn't open. After a James nod, Rob released the locks inside and Griz offered to help with the packages inside.

"Thanks, Bitsy said, I'm James' friend, Bitsy Schwartz."

"It's a pleasure ma'am, I'm Griz" Though she had never met everyone, Bitsy remembered those James had told her about though even he didn't know much about Griz. That he was friendly and helpful was the only thing she needed to know.

James carried several bags inside and sought out Harlene, who was opening the bar register. She greeted him with an eager grin.

"Howdy, glad you're here."

"I wanted to talk to you before the others come in. The chief of police informed me there wouldn't be any charges for attempted murder and no destruction of property penalty unless Tug insists. I don't believe he will."

"Tug is helping Cody in the back. I doubt he'd be doing that if he were planning on accusing me. He's a good natured man."

"Somehow I think his being here has nothing to do with his kind attitude. He is in love with you."

Harlene blushed.

"I know it. I'll never be worthy of him; though together we have a real good shot."

"There's a reason for celebration right there."

Bitsy entered the bar with Melody, Russ Jensen and Tori following through the door. James introduced everyone around and ordered beer as they found seats.

Finished in the back, Tug and Cory came out and greeted everyone. Tug sat at the bar near Harlene and Cody said a temporary goodbye for something important he had to do elsewhere.

After he left, Harlene explained, "He's been seeing Thomasina's girl. I think he went to get her."

Stevie and Wood showed up in western gear looking easy relaxed out of police uniforms. Beer flowed freely and the band entertained with a variety of country songs. Russ and Melody did their version of Blake Shelton's 'Ol Red'. *

Griz, surprisingly too, was great on Luke Combs' 'Beer Never Broke My Heart'. **

> * Blake Shelton, James "Bo" Bohan, Don Goodman, Mark Sherril, Bobby Braddock produced it
> ** Luke Combs, Randy Montana, Jonathon Singleton Scott Moffatt produced it.

Cody returned, guiding Sonia to the open microphone. Nobody knew Sonia sang, but then it's Nashville. They used a duet Taylor Swift and Luke Bryan entertained a Nashville audience with. "I Don't Want This Night to End". *** They sounded great together and everyone wanted to know how they pulled it together.

Cody said, "We practiced on the way here. Sonia is a very fast learner."

*** Luke Bryan, Dallas Davidson, Rhett Akins, Ben Hayslip, Capitol Records Nashville

Most everyone was paired off if you counted Russ and Melody as one couple and Stevie and Wood for another. The exception was Tori Calhoun. She wore an ornamented western top with tight jeans and boots, looking very good. Several men noticed when she walked in and whistled or said, "Hey Babe". She waved nonchalantly but otherwise ignored them. She sat with fellow officers and focused on a beer. The waitress flew by, depositing one beer token in front of her mason jar. Thinking James had bought that she inquired, "Who is responsible for this?"

Kaitlin, the server, indicated a booth in the back. It was Jamie Chase. Her heart did not stop as sometimes expressed in romance novels, but it sure fluttered. Just as she turned to say thank you, the band started into the music she intended to sing. She took the microphone from its stand and decided to sing standing up. Intending to do both Alison Krauss and Keith Whitley parts in the duet****, she started in singing.

> It's amazing how you can speak right to my heart
> Without saying a word you can light up the dark
> Try as I may I can never explain
> What I hear when you don't say a thing
> But just like in a real romance, Jamie took the microphone from her after that verse, finished and sang very sweetly,
> The smile on your face lets me know that you need me
> There's a truth in your eyes saying you'll never leave me
> Tori recovered and the two finished the song together,
> The touch of your hand says you'll catch me
> If ever I fall

Now you say it best
When you say nothing at all
****Songwriter Paul Overstreet. Don Schlitz, Keith Whitley recorded and Alison Krauss covered as tribute to Keith

Admiring reactions followed the finish, leading to enthusiastic applause or wolf whistles when Jamie kissed Tori in front of patrons, God and everyone else.

At Bitsy's request the band picked up and played "The Gambler". She gave out the albums she'd purchased.–Goo Goo Clusters for everyone too. Guests took that time for eating the excellent bar food while enjoying music. Melody stopped at each seat waiting for attention and scraps of food. She got plenty of both. Everyone admitted to having a wonderful time and packed up presents for leaving. James stood near the open door with light from outside highlighting his tall frame. Bitsy handed him the only gift bag left. He reached inside it, pulling out his gift that was a Jason Aldean signature hat- cowboy of course. He put it on exclaiming, "What do you think? It's Hollywood with a touch of twang?"

As if by magic, the jukebox started to play, "Crazy Town". James believed in magic happening, but he observed Bitsy on the phone. Touch tunes app? he thought. No she was transferring money for the bar bill. He looked up–across the bar he saw Tori's smiling face. She had played it. Everyone joined in singing the chorus of

"Everybody plays, everybody sings… We're all just trying to make it in this crazy town. ++ Jason Aldean "Crazy Town", Brett Jones and Rodney Clawson original songwriters Ole media Management original publishers, Wide Open Album release distributed by Eagle Rock."

James tipped his hat. "Here's hoping this talented bunch keeps playing on Music Row."

With no prompting, a song started up, "Murder on Music Row"–a George Strait/ Alan Jackson oldie–by itself it seemed. James only nodded and waved everyone out the exit acknowledging some things could not be explained.

Sketched Hat–Alexander Marshall Clemmens, Yaho, Japan, May 10, 2020 for Mother's Day

MURDER ON THE ICE FLOE IN NASHVILLE

Taper Tilman's interfering ways caused trouble. When he is strangled on the Cumberland River at TUG'S ICE FISHING, there are many suspects. Investigating detectives Lt. Eli James and Sgt. Tori Calhoun track the killer to Cumberland Bluffs, a mountain where the culprit plans to escape. Without much climbing experience, they go up the steep slopes to bring him down for Tilman's murder.

In 2013, stating on Smashwords, JB Clemmens released the book, Jigsaw. Since then nine more books were written, several appearing on Amazon, Primarily Fiction, Lieutenant James Mystery Series includes Mystery at PimaPoint and The Numbered Cups. Mystery, The historical book, Upon the Moon and Woodstock, about 1969, The Vietnam War, and The Culture then, has been released from Readers Magnet Publishing Firm. Jeanie has sung in choirs for many years and continues to enjoy country songs, reading and especially writing.

A NOVEL INSPIRED BY TRUE EVENTS

CALABRIA:
Mountains and Valleys

RAFFAELE ZUCCARELLI

AUTHOR